This book belongs to:

_____

_____

This edition published by Parragon Books Ltd in 2016 and distributed by

Parragon Inc.
440 Park Avenue South, 13th Floor
New York, NY 10016
www.parragon.com

Retold by Rachel Elliot
Illustrated by Charlotte Cooke
Designed by Kathryn Davies and Anna Madin

ISBN 978-1-4748-3377-6

Printed in China

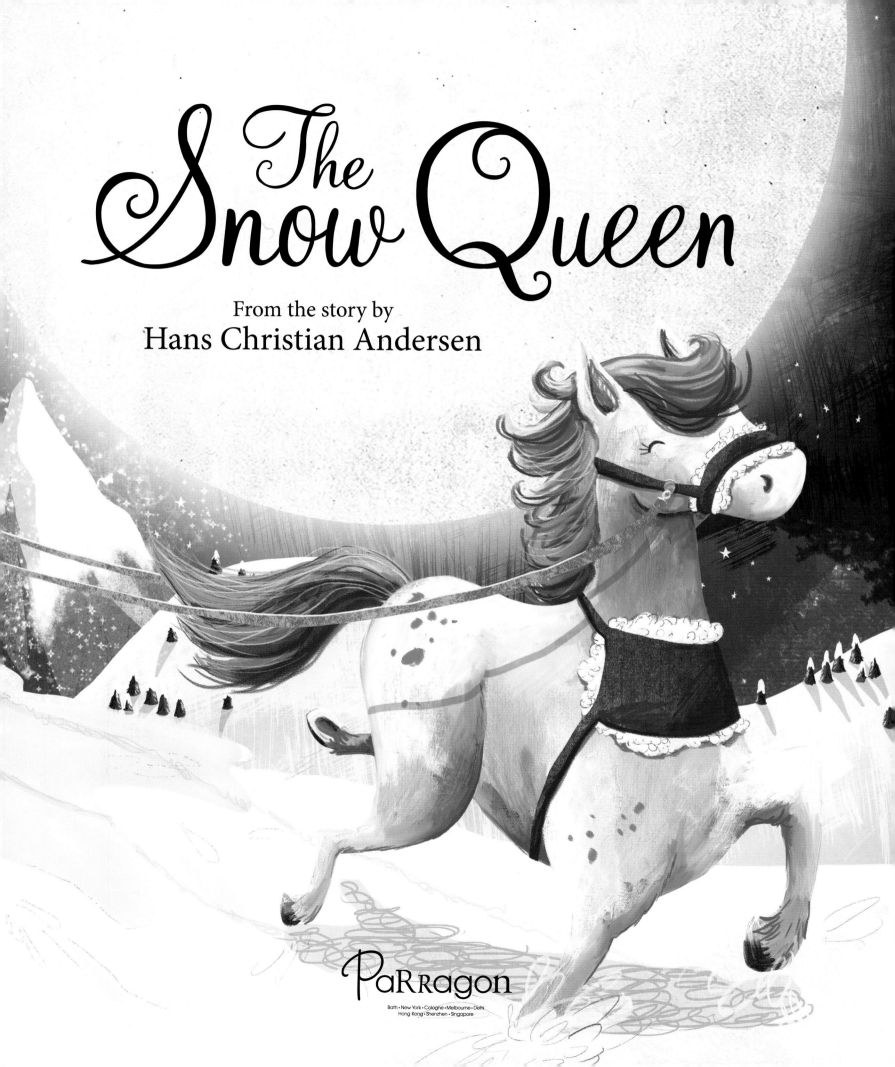

The Snow Queen

From the story by
Hans Christian Andersen

PaRRagon

Bath • New York • Cologne • Melbourne • Delhi
Hong Kong • Shenzhen • Singapore

Once, there was a wicked imp who made a magic mirror. Everything it reflected looked ugly and mean. The most beautiful princess would look dreadful. The sunniest day would seem rainy and cold.

One day, some careless sprites took the mirror, but it fell from their hands. It smashed into tiny specks, each no bigger than a grain of sand. The glass specks got into people's eyes and made everything look bad to them. Some specks became caught in people's hearts, making them feel cross and grumpy.

A few of the specks from the mirror floated toward a faraway place, where there lived two best friends and neighbors, named Gerda and Kay.

The pair spent endless days together. In the winter, Gerda's grandmother told them wonderful stories while the snow swirled outside.

"The Snow Queen brings the winter weather," she would say. "She peeps in at the windows and leaves icy patterns on the glass."

In the summer, the children would play in the little roof garden between their houses. One sunny day, they were reading together when Kay let out a cry.

"Ouch! I felt a pain in my chest, and now there is something in my eye!" he exclaimed. Specks from the imp's magic mirror had gotten caught in Kay's eye and his heart.

"These roses stink," he said with a frown.

Gerda couldn't understand why Kay was suddenly so cross.

Kay was bad-tempered throughout the summer and the fall, and was still cross when winter came. One snowy day, Kay stormed off with his sled, looking for ways he could cause some mischief.

Suddenly, a large white sleigh swept past, and Kay quickly hitched his sled to the back.

With a swoosh, Kay was off! The sleigh pulled him through the streets, faster and faster—out of the town and into the countryside.

When the sleigh finally stopped, a majestic figure turned slowly toward Kay. He couldn't believe his eyes—it was the Snow Queen from Gerda's grandmother's story! The queen kissed Kay's forehead and her icy touch froze Kay's heart. He forgot all about Gerda and his home.

Gerda missed Kay. She searched all through the town and
then down by the river, but Kay wasn't there. Just as she was
about to give up, Gerda noticed a little boat among the rushes.
"Perhaps the river will carry me to Kay," she thought.
She climbed in and the boat glided away.

Gerda floated along for many hours, until at last, the boat reached the shore.

A large raven came hopping toward her.

"Hello," he croaked. "Where are you going, little girl?"

Gerda was amazed to hear the raven speak, but he seemed kind, so she told him about Kay.

"I think I have seen your friend," the raven said. "A young man that sounds like him has married a princess close by. My sister lives at the palace. She could take you to him."

That night, the raven's sister led Gerda
up a narrow staircase to the palace bedroom
where the prince and princess slept.
Gerda lifted her lamp.
"Kay!" she called excitedly. "It's me, Gerda!"
The prince opened his eyes and gazed at
her in surprise—but he wasn't Kay.

Poor Gerda! She was hungry and far from home.
She told the prince and princess her story,
and the princess hugged her.

"Let us help you," she said. "Sleep here
tonight, and tomorrow you can continue your
journey in comfort."

The next morning, Gerda was given warm clothes and a golden sleigh. She set off into the woods, but before long, she was spotted by a band of robbers.

"That carriage is pure gold!" they hissed.

The robbers sprang out and captured Gerda, ready to take her away to their castle.

Suddenly, the daughter of the robber chief appeared. Her hair was tangled and her eyes were black as coal. The girl was lonely and excited by the thought of a new friend.

"Please, treat her gently!" the robber girl pleaded. "She can stay with me."

The robbers' castle was guarded by
mean-looking bulldogs. Magpies and crows
squawked from the crumbling battlements.
Gerda was grateful to the robber girl
for her kindness. She would have been very
scared if she'd been all alone.

Inside, Gerda met the robber girl's pigeons and her pet reindeer. Gerda told her new friend about Kay.

That night, as the girls slept, the pigeons began to coo.

"Gerda, we have seen Kay," said the pigeons. "He was traveling to Lapland with the Snow Queen, under her spell."

Gerda sat up, feeling hopeful again.

"I know the way to the Snow Queen's palace," added the reindeer.

Gerda woke the robber girl and told her what the animals had said. The robber girl quickly untied the reindeer.

"Take Gerda to Lapland," she said. "She must find her friend."

It was a long, cold journey, but at last Gerda and the
reindeer arrived in Lapland. They stopped at a crooked little
cottage. The wise old woman who lived there knew all about Kay.

"Can you help Gerda defeat the Snow Queen?" the reindeer
quietly asked the wise woman, as Gerda sat by the fire.

The wise woman shook her head. "Gerda doesn't need my help,"
she whispered. "Her love for her friend is strong enough."

The next morning, the reindeer carried Gerda to the edge of the Snow Queen's garden. He set her down, and she started to run through the snow toward the palace.

Inside the ice palace, the beautiful Snow Queen still held Kay under her spell.

As she sat on her throne, the Snow Queen watched as Kay struggled to fit together some pieces of ice.

"You can go free when you have completed my puzzle," the Snow Queen told him. "All you have to do is spell out the word 'Eternity.'"

No matter how many times he tried to solve
the puzzle, Kay could not spell the word.

"Spring is coming," said the Snow Queen, suddenly, and she rose from her throne in a great hurry. "It is time for me to make it snow on the other side of the world!" She flew off in her sleigh, leaving Kay alone. At that moment, Gerda crept into the palace.

"Kay!" Gerda cried. She ran to her friend and hugged him. Her tears fell onto his chest. They melted his cold heart and washed away the speck of glass. Kay began to cry, too, and his tears washed the glass from his eye.

"Gerda!" Kay shouted in excitement.

The children's joy made the puzzle pieces dance among the spikes of ice. When the pieces settled again, they spelled out the word "Eternity," freeing Kay from the Snow Queen's spell.

The reindeer carried Gerda and Kay away from the palace to the edge of Lapland, where the snow disappeared.
"This is the start of spring," said the reindeer. "And now I must say goodbye."
"Goodbye, and thank you!" said Gerda and Kay.

As the reindeer left, someone rode out of the trees on a
beautiful horse and waved to them. It was the robber girl.

Gerda went to meet her, and they hugged each other happily.

"I am glad that you found Kay," she said. "I must go now,
but one day I will visit you."

Gerda and Kay walked for days on end. The spring flowers bloomed and blossomed, and when at last they heard the church bells ringing, they knew they were close to home.

"Grandmother!" called Gerda. "We're back at last!"

She ran up the stairs with Kay and found her grandmother sitting in the sunshine, reading her book. The old lady wrapped them in her arms and hugged them tightly.

"I knew that you would come home one day," she said.

They sat together in the little roof garden and told Gerda's grandmother all about their adventures.

Each year the Snow Queen brought the winter weather.

And each year, when the snow swirled outside, Kay and Gerda stayed safe and warm inside, listening to Gerda's grandmother's wonderful stories.